# The Key into Winter

### Janet S. Anderson
PAINTINGS BY **David Soman**

ALBERT WHITMAN & COMPANY · Morton Grove, Illinois

Library of Congress Cataloging-in-Publication Data
Anderson, Janet S. 1946-
The key into winter / Janet S. Anderson;
paintings by David Soman.
p.    cm.
Summary: Clara's mother tells the story of how,
as a young girl, she hid the key into winter,
in an attempt to stop the seasons from changing
and thus save her dying grandmother.
ISBN 0-8075-4170-2
[1. Seasons—Fiction. 2. Death—Fiction.
3. Grandmothers—Fiction.]
I. Soman, David, ill. II. Title.
PZ7.A5365Ke 1994                          93-13017
[E]—dc20                    CIP                    AC

The text of this book is set in Italia Medium.
The illustrations are rendered in watercolor.
Design by Susan B. Cohn.

This story was first published in the
September 1989 issue of *Cricket* Magazine.

*For my grandmother, Mary Clough Smith.* J.S.A.
*To Noah, my brother.* D.S.

**T**ell me, Mama," said Clara. "Tell me
again about the time you hid the key
into winter." She settled more snugly
into her mother's lap. Her grandmother
dozed beside them in a big chair.

Above them all, over the hearth, hung
four keys. The first was the key into spring.
It was made of silver, delicate and shining.
Next hung the key into summer, golden,
heavy, and gleaming. Beside it, the key into
autumn shone with a coppery glow. Last
was the key into winter. All the light of the
room burned in its crystal depths.

"Tell me again how you almost lost it forever," said Clara.

"Again?" said her mother. But she smiled. "It happened long ago, when I was very young."

"Younger than me?" said Clara.

"Younger than you," said her mother. "But even then, the keys hung over the hearth as they do today. I loved to look at them. And each season when my grandmother took one down, she let me hold it for a moment in my hand."

"How did it feel?" said Clara.

"You tell me," said her mother.

Clara shut her eyes to think. "The key into spring feels cool at first and then warms in your hand. The key into summer is hot, but it doesn't hurt. The key into autumn—"

"My favorite," said her mother.

"Not mine," said Clara. "It's like a shock, like sparks that glow and then disappear into the dark."

"And the key into winter?" said her mother.

Clara shivered. "It burns with cold down to my bones. I don't like it, Mama."

"I didn't like it, either," said her mother. "And one year, I decided I would hide it so that winter would never come."

"Tell me, Mama," said Clara.

And her mother told her.

It was a beautiful autumn. The trees glowed, even by moonlight. The barn was filled with a rich harvest: golden corn, yellow squash, orange pumpkins, red apples. Everything was bursting with color. It should have been a season of joy.

But instead, we were sad. My grandmother lay thin and quiet in her upstairs room. She still smiled, but she could no longer laugh or tell me the stories I loved to hear. The doctor would just shake his head and say, "There's not much I can do. Her body is old and tired. I'm afraid that this autumn will be her last."

Her last! But I loved her! There must be a way to save her!

Well, there was. It was easy. With my grandmother so sick, my mother was keeper of the keys now. She could stop the autumn from ending by not letting winter begin. But when I asked her, she shook her head. "Winter must come, Mattie," she said.

"Please," I begged her. "Don't use that ugly key into winter. Then autumn will stay, and Grandmother will stay. She'll laugh and tell me stories again."

But my mother just repeated her words. "Winter must come," she said, and that was all she would say.

The days passed. Each night the dark came earlier. Each morning my grandmother seemed weaker. What could I do? One morning I stared up at the key waiting coldly over the hearth. Just a single night remained before it would lock us out of one season and into another. There was no more time to lose.

That night, while everyone slept, I crept downstairs. Quietly, I pulled the stool over to the hearth. I stretched high on my toes to reach the key. It burned like cold fire in my hand. Wrapping it in a fold of my nightgown, I stumbled into the kitchen.

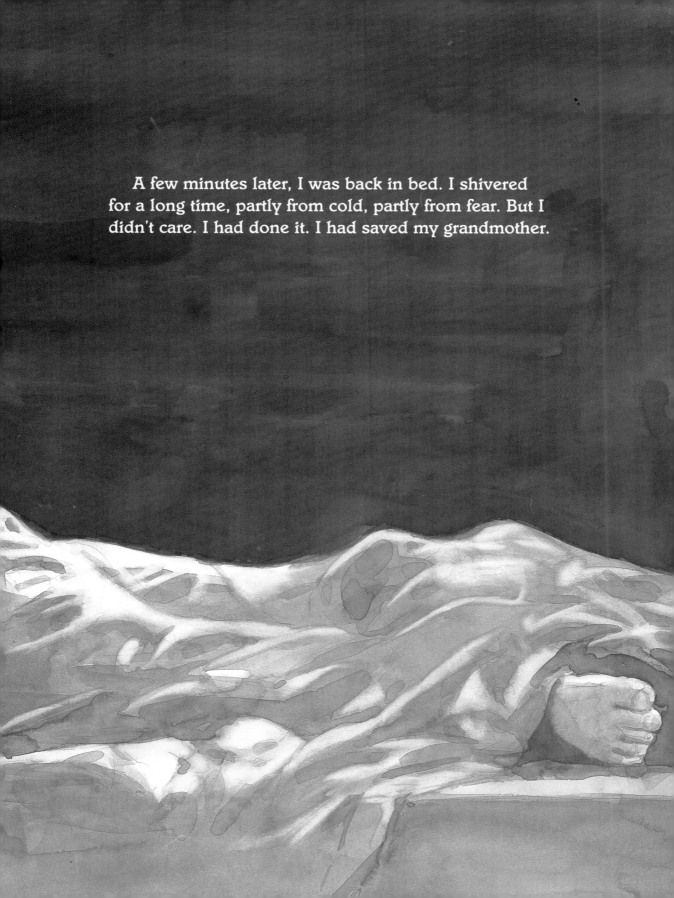

A few minutes later, I was back in bed. I shivered for a long time, partly from cold, partly from fear. But I didn't care. I had done it. I had saved my grandmother.

The next morning when I came downstairs, my
mother said nothing. But her face was stern, and in her
hands she held a Christmas ornament from our tree.

The tree! Why, it was nearly bare, and the tall white
candles from the mantel were lying in a heap on the
floor.

"Why are you taking down Christmas?" I asked.

"The key into winter is gone," she said. "Without
winter, there can be no Christmas."

I ran outside. The sleds and the ice skates pulled out weeks earlier by my impatient brothers were gone. My youngest brother was leaning against the barn. "I want snow," he was sobbing. "I want Christmas! I want winter!"

Inside the barn stood my father and my grandfather. They were looking at the plow and the bags of seed corn and at the wooden buckets for collecting sap from our old maples. "A terrible thing," my grandfather was saying. "No winter, no spring."

"No summer," said my father. "No harvest. A terrible thing."

Frantic, I ran back inside and up to my grandmother's room. I knelt down beside her bed. "It's not a terrible thing, is it?" I whispered to her. "Who cares about Christmas? With no winter, you'll soon be well again, won't you? Won't you?"

But my grandmother barely opened her eyes. Her voice was very weak. "No winter? No chance, then, for one more spring." And she closed her eyes again.

"Mama!" I screamed, but she was already there.

"She's asleep," she said. "It's all right."

"Mama!" I cried. "Can't you bring spring now?" I tugged her down the stairs and pointed up at the silvery key. "Please take it down. Turn it. That's what Grandmother is waiting for. She's waiting for the spring to make her well."

"Listen to me," said my mother. "The key alone won't work. The key would unlock the door, yes, but only winter can open it. Only winter can open the door into spring."

"I hid the key, Mama," I said. "I hid the key into winter."

"I know," she said.

"I hid it in the stove," I sobbed. "It's melted now, I'm sure it is."

"Show me," said my mother.

Together we went into the kitchen. I opened the
door of the stove. There, deep among the flames,
was a glowing shape. With her long tongs, my
mother reached in and pulled it out. "It didn't melt!"
I whispered.

"Don't touch it," said my mother. "Its cold now would freeze your very blood." She looked at me gravely. "And so what shall I do with it, with this key into winter?"

I scrunched my eyes shut. "Is tonight the night?" I finally asked.

"Tonight is the night," she said.
"Winter must come?"
"You tell me."
I thought of my grandmother and wiped my tear-streaked face. "I guess only winter can open the door into spring," I said.

Late that night, as we all gathered in front of the hearth, my father gently carried my grandmother down the stairs. She looked up at the familiar keys and smiled faintly. Then she opened her hand. My mother placed the crystal key into it, and together they turned the key into winter.

For a moment, Clara and her mother sat silently.

"*Was* it her last autumn?" Clara asked.

"Yes," said her mother, "but she lived to see another spring."

Clara looked over at the big chair beside her. "Grandmother?" she whispered.

The old woman opened her eyes, then stretched her fingers and reached for her knitting. She pointed one long needle at the four shining keys. "It'll be many a year before you get to turn them, Clara. You *or your* mother. Come here now and hold this wool for me."

As Clara's mother went into the kitchen, Clara settled on a stool beside her grandmother, and the old woman handed her the wool. Then her fingers closed around Clara's.

"So you don't want summer to end, eh, child?" she said. "No more playing and swimming, just school and work?" She gave a low laugh. "When I was your age, I felt the same way."

"You?" asked Clara, astonished. "You did?"

"Yes," said her grandmother. "Now, get on with this wool, and I'll tell you about the time I almost lost the key into autumn."